QUANDARIES

QUANDARIES:

Short Stories to Make You Wonder

Henry W. Prunckun

Bibliologica Press

Disclaimer

This is a work of fiction. The characters, incidents and dialogues in this book are of the author's imagination and are not to be construed as real. Any resemblance to actual events or people, living or dead, is coincidental.

Quandaries:
Short Stories to Make You Wonder
by Henry W. Prunckun

ISBN 978-0-6456209-8-6

 A catalogue record for this
book is available from the
NATIONAL LIBRARY OF AUSTRALIA
National Library of Australia

Bibliologica Press
P.O. Box 656
Unley, South Australia, 5061
Australia

CONTENTS

Dedication....................vii

Kneel 1

A Small Contribution...........5

Gone Fishing..................9

Do You Know Who I Am?............15

Birthday Lunch 19

A Lesson in Strength............25

Strawberries 31

Charcoal Grey Clouds............33

Richter's Proposition 39

There're Hundreds of Them 55

Someone I Once Knew..............57

Delirium 63

Newcomb's Daughters 67

The Dick.................81

The Expanding Universe 89

Abilene's Fog.................93

Beyond What We Can See 99

About the Author 103

DEDICATION

~ I Chose Ann ~

I might have been another man.
I might have lived in another land.
But I chose to be who I am.
I chose to live here with Ann.

This poem is about my wife, Ann E. Doolette. It was originally published as part of the *Raining Poetry in Adelaide* project (conducted by Facculty of Arts, University of Adelaide, 2017).

KNEEL

As the disclaimer to this book says, "Any resemblance to actual events or people, living or dead, is completely coincidental." And this is true. But stories must be grounded in the real world; otherwise, they will not be believed. Therefore, stories are amalgams of observations of actual happenings but have been subjected to the writer's imagination. This is a charming story based on one such event.

~ ~ ~

Walking across the lobby of the stone building lacked the sensation of wind on my face, but I still felt like I was falling, plummeting to earth. Although I'd never parachuted, when I stepped through those foyer doors, it was as if I was jumping out of an aircraft. I understood why skydiving never appealed to me.

The adrenalin pumping through my veins made me shake. I felt out of place, so when the waiter appeared offering us drinks, I didn't need prompting; I clutched a white wine.

"Take a breath. He's only a judge," said Loretta Ho.

I'm sure she thought her advice would comfort me, but it only made me feel worse.

This story was originally published by Celapene Press (Melbourne, Australia: pp. 7–9) in Katheryn Duncan, editor, *Short and Twisted, 2016* when I used the pen name of Oliver Yardley.

"It's okay for you," I said. "You're the firm's senior partner. The two of you probably studied law together at college. I'm a legal associate."

"Young woman, you're *my* legal associate. And a very capable one. That's why you're at this meeting."

"Meeting? I thought we were having drinks to… Well, anyway, I've never appeared in a courtroom, not even for a parking violation. It gives me a nosebleed being in the grandeur of this social club."

"Well, it's just as well it's not a courtroom then. We'll no doubt talk a bit of commercial law, but for the record, this is social. A chance encounter with a judge." She offered her arm to me the way an aunt might.

I seized it and gulped a mouthful of wine, trying not to teeter on my high heels as we walked into the wood-paneled drawing room.

There was the light scent of polished oak. I could hear a murmur coming from a couple of groups of people at the other ends of the room and the clinking of silverware on bone china plates from a couple seated in a pair of leather chesterfields.

Judge Wilkinson was by the fireplace. A log flickered flames over a bed of glowing embers. The warmth was inviting. He stood holding a glass of Scotch, ice cubes still visible. But the two men on either side of him had empty tumblers. They looked ready for refills.

As we joined the circle, the judge was finishing a story. "So, I asked counsel—casually—how he arrived at that conclusion. You should have seen his facial expression; it said it all."

The two men laughed. Appearing satisfied with the

execution of his punch line, Judge Wilkinson took a sip, rolled the ice around, and then held up his glass in a sign of mock victory.

I didn't know the context but could surmise: some junior lawyer got a roasting in his court.

Loretta interjected, "Gentlemen, I'd like to introduce my legal associate, Janice Carlsen." And with a composed sweep of her hand, she offered me center stage.

I nodded, and fighting a quaking voice, I managed to say, "Your Honor. Gentlemen."

Judge Wilkinson's eyes met mine. They were a steely gray. Piercing. He spoke just one word. "Kneel."

Without hesitation, I did, bowing my head as I would when entering court. When I looked up, the judge's eyes were wide with amazement.

I stood. My hand holding the glass trembled.

He leaned toward me, shook his head slightly then in a casual voice—the one I imagined he used to address counsel—he repeated himself, "Kneel."

Like a fishing bobber, I went down on one knee, this time staying put. Then, Loretta's hand touched my arm.

My eyes met Judge Wilkinson's. He was waving to me to rise, palms upward, nearly spilling the remains of his drink. "No, no. Please, Ms Carlsen, don't do that."

The murmur had stopped. There was no clinking.

With a helpful tug from Loretta, I rose, my toes curling in my shoes. I snapped my mouth shut, fearing I would stutter something stupid.

I heard the whisper of Loretta's voice. "His name's Neil. He's inviting you to address him by his first name."

A SMALL CONTRIBUTION

Could the frustration of a collector soliciting money for the upkeep of a local swimming pool be something else? Could he be a hustler trying to con an older person out of cash? Could this woman be wise to his trick, turning the table on him? You decide.

~ ~ ~

"Oh, hello. What can I do for you?"

"Good morning, ma'am. I'm collecting for the local swimming pool. We're trying to keep it open for the kids."

"Oh? I thought you might be with the— Hmm, who are they?"

"Not sure who you mean."

"You know, those nice people who come around and read the scriptures?"

"The Mormons?"

"What do they believe in?"

"Don't know."

"Well, how can you read from the Holy Book then?"

"I'm not here for that; I'm collecting for the pool."

"Ah, they're not Mormons. They're Jehovah's Witnesses."

This story was first published under my pseudonym of Oliver Yardley in Katheryn Duncan, editor, *Short and Twisted, 2017* (Knoxfield, Victoria: Celapene Press), pp. 49–50.

"Okay, I'll take your word for it. But are you able to contribute?"

"You see, young man, if my memory serves me correctly, which it doesn't all the time— Mind you, it did once. When I was younger, your age, I could recall facts and figures and—"

"Yes, I believe you. But do you want to donate to the pool?"

"The pool?"

"Yes, that's why I'm here. The local pool. For the kids."

"I have children. They loved to swim when they were young. They're all adults now. I'm a grandmother. Six grandchildren. Did you know that?"

"Well then, you'll appreciate the importance of this collection."

"Dear me! Of course I do. I may not remember many things, but I know about children. They like being read to. Me too, by those people who come around— Who are they again?"

"The Jehovah's?"

"So, you *are* a Jehovah's Witness? Come in."

"No, no, I'm collecting for the pool. Are you able to make a small contribution?"

"To the swimming pool?"

"Yes."

"Certainly. Wait a minute; I'll be right back— Here you are. Do you have something to put it in?"

"A glass of water?"

"You did say a *small* contribution."

GONE FISHING

I want to say I'm being honest when I say that the kernel of this story is grounded in fact, but because I write fiction, all I can say is what we hear as the truth may have a backstory to it.

~ ~ ~

A client came to me about a week ago. He said he wanted to meet at a coffee shop the day after next to discuss a sensitive matter. I told him I didn't work Sundays. But he insisted and said he'd pay for the first consultation; the offer I made to all potential clients was no charge for the first consult. My husband and daughter were camping for the weekend, and my daughter's monthly orthodontic payment was due soon, so I agreed.

When I arrived, he was seated at a table against the wall. He appeared to be part of the establishment: traditional, a conformist. His gray hair gave him a soft, fatherly appearance, and he drank black coffee. Everything about him seemed normal. Nevertheless, something struck me as odd.

He looked sad. Or was it the sentimental appearance of an artist? Who knows? The point is, he didn't appear a conspiracy theorist. Then again, I'm not sure there's a profile for them. I've had widows tell me that their dead husbands were trying to contact them through aliens, and I had a young man claim that government secret police were trying to steal his brain so they could use it to crack North Korean ciphers.

9

He briefed me on the job—he suspected his wife of infidelity. I had given up on being surprised when I heard people say they thought their spouses were cheating. Or their business partners were diddling them out of their share of the profits. Anyway, this guy wanted proof either way.

I said, "I can only collect evidence if she's unfaithful. I can't provide proof of fidelity."

He recognized the difference and apologized for his error in logic. When he spoke, he presented as a gentleman and well-educated.

I said, "I work on the five-by-five principle. Five hours of surveillance usually gives me five minutes of actionable intelligence or evidence." I pointed out the process was like fishing, and like fishing, there were no guarantees. "It could turn out to be five-by-zero."

He nodded, placed cash for our meeting and five hours of surveillance into a folded napkin, and then slid it across the table.

I put the parcel in my pocket after advising him that I needed to do a few background checks on him first to assure myself that he wasn't using me to cause this woman harm. It wasn't what he said to that statement because he didn't say anything; it was the look he gave me. It unsettled me. Infidelity cases always end in tears. I had a suspicion that this one would follow that pattern.

I had my coffee and read the newspaper at Perotti's espresso bar on Monday morning. When I finished, I got out my Netbook and ran my checks. It turned out that he was a federal court judge. Before being elevated to the bench, he practiced in commercial and contractual matters in the civil jurisdiction. His wife—and it turned out that she was his wife—was a medical practitioner. She ran a general practice in one of the leafy suburbs. No doubt specializing in Botox treatments...

Assured the case didn't have links to alien abductions, brain-stealing cryptographers, or stalkers, I headed out to recon the couple's house.

Like fishing, you can cast your line and sit all day. Or you can throw your line in and get a nibble within minutes. As I drove down the street, I saw his wife's Benz reversing out of the driveway and heading toward the local shopping mall.

I had a nibble.

I followed her, watched her park, and then tailed her as she wandered the shops. At an open-air café, she ordered one of those healthy drinks. A man half her age approached. They greeted and talked briefly. They looked like friends or perhaps medical colleagues. He didn't appear to be a patient; the body language was wrong. Nevertheless, I pressed the shutter release and captured a half-dozen frames, just in case.

He departed, and a few minutes later, so did she. But in those final minutes, while she drank, she looked anxious. She glanced around a lot. Her casualness appeared forced. She seemed to want to leave but was waiting. For what?

When she did, I followed her Benz to a wealthy suburban address. I drove past the house where she had parked. I activated my dashcam and recorded a few stills of her car in the driveway. There was another car next to hers—its license plate was in full view. But so far, none of this suggested anything untoward; all could be easily explained.

Ninety minutes later, I landed my fish.

From my location down the street, I took a photo of her hanging off his six-foot frame as they exited the house. He was the man from the café. Her head was on his chest, gazing up at his eyes. They stopped in the driveway next to their cars, and her right leg wrapped around his left. They kissed, her hand on his crouch; his fingers spread over her fleshy bottom, and my camera captured it all in twenty-megapixel detail.

I put the camera away and drove off. I didn't need to write a report for this case. There was no need to file a surveillance log, nor produce an itemized list of expenses. I just needed a couple of well-selected photos to tell the story.

I printed the images on glossy paper at my office and phoned the client. Later that afternoon, I slid an envelope across the café table. I labeled it "Photos of my fishing trip." He didn't open it—he just thanked me.

As he walked away, I didn't think he was appreciative. I think he wanted me to prove that she was faithful.

On Tuesday morning, I ordered my usual morning espresso. I read the newspaper and discussed the government's proposed tax changes with the waiter.

On page three, I saw a photo of yesterday's target being interviewed outside a private hospital. The caption said that Judge Pearson of the Federal Appeals Court had died after mistakenly taking the wrong medication: "Not even the quick actions of his wife—who was also his treating physician—could save him."

The article said his wife had been providing medical care for work-related stress—high caseloads and lengthy court hours. The article talked about how he had faithfully served the legal community for decades and cited many noble things he had done during his time in the law.

The article concluded that his wife found it particularly sad because he was talking about retiring. She told the reporter that he had met with a friend just the other day to discuss a *fishing trip*.

Reading those words caused a chill to run down my spine. For sure, she had found the photos.

Recalling the expression on the judge's face made me conclude it wasn't sadness or sentimentality—it was concern.

I reread the sentence, "Took the wrong medication." Was that a medical euphemism for suicide, or could his doctor wife have...?

DO YOU KNOW WHO I AM?

This story is about holding your nerve and thinking fast to get yourself out of a potentially career-ending situation.

~ ~ ~

"Asha, you can use this office while the carpenters finish refurbishing the open-plan offices."

"Neat! Someone important must sit here—look at that city view!"

It's the Managing Director's office. You'll report to her when she returns from vacation on Thursday. In the meantime, enjoy the comforts; they won't last long."

"Oh, I will!

Asha, a newly hired software engineer in her first job since graduating with her computer science degree, surveyed the office. Her thoughts drifted to the sign on the door that showed her boss's name and entertained the idea that one day, her name—Asha Singh—would appear on an office door.

Her gaze settled on the desk phone. It had five preset buttons at the bottom of the device, each with a person's last name on it. Concluding that the one on the far left must be the boss's assistant, Asha lifted the handset and pressed the button.

A man's voice answered within a few rings, "Van Dijk."

15

Asha spoke into the mouthpiece using a tone she thought was keeping with a future MD, "Can you get me a coffee, black, no sugar."

There was silence.

She repeated herself, "Can you get me a coffee, black, no sugar."

The voice on the end of the phone bellowed, "Do you know who *I* am?"

Asha said, "No."

The voice shouted, "I'm the President of this company!"

She cleared her throat, "Do you know who *I* am?"

Still panting from his outburst, he said, "No."

A smile appeared on Asha's face, "Good," and she placed the handset in its cradle.

BIRTHDAY LUNCH

Now, how could any writer come up with such a story? Well, indeed, not this writer. I changed the names and places and admit that none of what was said was actually spoken, but two sisters of Polish immigrants did have a Sunday outing to a "restaurant" like this, where they made themselves tomato soup. This story is dedicated to the memories of Anna and Marian.

~ ~ ~

I asked for a black coffee at the take-out counter.

"Sugar?"

"No thanks." I pushed across a crisp bill.

He pushed back a paper cup of coffee and my change.

I scooped up what was left of the ten.

"Before your break, Officer, would you evict those two vagrants?"

My gaze followed his finger across the café to two young girls. They sat on stools that faced the serving counter in a typical diner style. A napkin dispenser, salt and pepper shakers, and condiments in squeeze bottles rested along the white Formica-topped counter.

"They're underage," he continued. "Can't be in a restaurant without a parent."

I looked around, taking in what he considered to be a *restaurant*.

"No doubt from a single-parent family," he muttered. Or, more like a—"

I cut him off. "There's no law against being in an eating establishment without a parent." I couldn't recall that section of the criminal law, but I was stalling, wanting to see where he was heading.

"They're wasting my time, taking up seats that paying customers could be at."

I looked back at the empty entrance. "You're referring to the line of patrons waiting to come in?"

"Not the point. They ordered two mugs of hot water. Been sitting there for fifteen minutes. They need to buy something or leave."

I brought out my spiral pad and penciled a few notes. "Let's see: thirteen hundred hours, owner complaining about two girls not ordering food." I looked up. "How old are the perpetrators? I guess that the older one is ten or eleven. The younger one, perhaps six?"

He folded his arms, pushing out his chest.

I picked up my coffee and walked over to them, sliding onto the stool next to the older child to their left. "Hello, ladies. Mind if I join you?"

Their shoes were brown, scuffed, and hadn't seen a recent polish. They had jeans, the younger one in an overall style. The older girl had on a russet-colored sweater; the younger had her hair tied back in a single ponytail. Although not wearing the latest fashion, they were neat, clean, and looked well.

I told them my name and asked theirs. The little one stiffened and looked away.

The older girl reached for the menu, pretending to read. "We're trying to decide what to order."

The tomato sauce dispenser caught my eye. I surveyed the trail of drips that led to their mugs. "Yea, it's difficult to choose. So many things on the menu."

I saw evidence of salt and pepper sprinkles around the mugs. Two empty cellophane packets of the complimentary crackers were in attendance.

"I'm sure you'll select something delicious. In the meantime, you're enjoying your tomato soup."

"It's our 'starter'," the older girl said.

She went back to studying the menu, her face mimicking an expression of concentration. The younger girl inched toward the older one until she balanced on the edge of her stool.

I nodded. "Well, it's been a pleasure talking to you two young ladies, but…" I opened my leather jacket, exposing my sidearm and handcuffs.

The little one gasped.

"I need to keep patroling." I withdrew my wallet and placed a bill on the counter. "Would you allow me to buy you lunch in repayment for your company?"

The two moved away slightly. "We're not allowed to take anything from people we don't know."

The little one spoke for the first time and with firmness in her voice. "Dad said."

"Well, your father's right. You should always be cautious. But I'm not a stranger. You know my name; besides, a police officer is everyone's friend."

They looked at each other.

21

"Sounds like your father looks after you well. Where's he now?"

"At work. He drives a bus."

"So, your Sunday afternoon job is to look after your younger sister?"

"It's her birthday."

"So, you've taken her out for lunch. Well, then, you'll have time for dessert too."

I placed a second bill on the table, and the little one's eyes widened. With my coffee in hand, I slid off the stool and started for the door.

"My name's Anna. She's Marian."

Their last name sounded Polish. I smiled at them and said, "Don't forget to leave a tip."

A LESSON IN STRENGTH

Strength and wisdom, when wielded responsibly, can be powerful in self-defense and protection. However, the true measure of their worth lies not in the harm they can cause, but in the values and lessons they uphold. This story reminds us that empowerment should always be balanced with empathy, and unity within a family can be strengthened by the values we pass down through the generations.

~ ~ ~

Hank stirred the simmering spaghetti sauce, his eyes lingering over the bubbling pot with a mixture of focus and nostalgia. The kitchen counter was a still-life of culinary staples: onions, garlic, tomatoes, and various herbs and spices. As he reached for the wooden spoon, his gaze caught his ten-year-old grandson, Archie, silently doodling in a notebook at the kitchen table.

"What's troubling you, Archie?" Hank inquired, the concern edging his voice.

Archie glanced up; his eyes clouded. "It's nothing, Grandpa," he murmured before returning to his scribbling.

Sensing the gravity of his grandson's mood, Hank laid the wooden spoon beside the pot and walked over. He gently placed his arm around Archie, "You've got that look on your face, the same one your mom used to have when she was your age. Is something wrong at school?"

Archie's eyes met the notebook below him, and a tear fell onto the pages. "Some kids are giving me a hard time, Grandpa."

Hank's jaw tightened. "Have you told those guys to 'shove off'?"

"Mom says fighting isn't the answer."

Hank looked at his daughter, Naomi, who just entered the kitchen. She was strong-willed, a characteristic he both admired and was frustrated by.

"Naomi, what's this about Archie being bullied at school?"

Naomi addressed her father as "Dad" when she wanted something, "Daddy" when she was buttering him up to ask a big favor, and "Hank" when she was telling him off.

"*Hank*, there's always another way," Naomi argued. "Violence is never the solution."

Hank shook his head. "There's a difference between offense and defense, Naomi. The Bible says, "Don't be afraid of them. Remember the Lord—who is great and awesome—and fight for your families, your sons and your daughters, your wives, and your homes."

"That sermon is rich coming from an atheist! How would you know what the Bible says?" she said.

"I read widely."

"As far as I know, you are making that up like when you read stories to us as kids? You'd make up the words as you'd flipped the pages."

Hank fixed his daughter in his gaze, "I have to teach him how to stand up for himself."

Naomi's lips tightened. "*Hank*, the Bible also tells you to turn the other cheek."

* * *

Every Saturday morning for the next several weeks, the ritual between Archie and his grandfather unfolded with a sense of regularity. As the world outside woke up to the weekend, Archie would arrive at his grandparent's home, greeted by the warm aroma of his grandma's muffins and pancakes and the comfort of old family photos adorning the walls.

Without a word, Hank would retrieve the key from the top drawer of a wooden credenza, and together, they would walk to the garage, a sanctuary where time seemed to stand still, and wisdom was passed down like a family heirloom.

Unlocking the door, Hank would slide it open to reveal an organized space filled with tools that had seen better days, scraps of wood, and memorabilia from his children's youthful adventures.

A worn-out punching bag and a pair of boxing gloves stood in one corner, hanging as if waiting for this moment. Hank would call these weekend sessions Archie's "life lessons." Although they involved physical techniques, Archie knew they were laden with metaphors for more significant battles in life.

The lessons started with foundational stances, the bedrock of defense. Hank would stand across from Archie, his eyes narrowing as he corrected a misplaced foot or adjusted the angle of Archie's arms. "Balance is key, buddy. Without it, you're as good as down," Hank would say, his voice imbued with the seriousness that came from his experience as a former police officer and prison guard.

They began with basic postures, gradually progressing to blocking techniques and counterpunches. Hank took his time, ensuring that Archie learned the physical movements and the philosophy of self-defense. "Anticipate, plan, and act," he'd say, stressing the mental aspects of defense as much as the physical ones. "You have to think ahead, anticipate what's coming, and plan your move," he'd say, watching Archie's eyes light up as the young boy deflected Hank's simulated attack.

At first, Archie was hesitant, the weight of his grandfather's teachings heavy on his young shoulders. But with each session, he began to internalize the physical movements and the thinking behind them. He felt a newfound sense of control and empowerment, a feeling that he was not just reacting to the world but capable of shaping his fate.

"Remember, Archie, this is about defense, not attack," Hank would remind him, locking eyes with his grandson as if to etch the words into his subconscious. "You never instigate; you never seek trouble. But when trouble finds you, and it will, you stand your ground when there's no alternative."

Holding his grandfather's gaze, Archie nodded with a maturity beyond his ten years. "I understand, Grandpa," he replied, the importance of the lessons settling within him, preparing him for the uncertainties of life ahead.

* * *

Naomi had the rare afternoon off from work, so she decided to pick Archie up from school and take him to his favorite place—the local library. She parked her car and walked towards the schoolyard. What she saw next took her breath away: Archie was cornered in the playground, surrounded by a group of boys, and his back to the fence.

Her blood boiled as she saw the ring-leader, a tall kid named Ivan, close his fists and pull back his arm. Naomi started running, but before she could reach them, Archie moved.

It was a fluid, swift motion, almost poetic. Archie blocked Ivan's blow and delivered a quick, calculated strike to the bully's stomach. Ivan crumbled, gasping for air.

Naomi stopped in her tracks, eyes wide, heart pounding. A teacher appeared, finally, and dispersed the group.

* * *

As Naomi and Archie walked toward the car, the tension was palpable. Finally, Naomi broke the silence.

"Did Grandpa teach you those moves?" she asked.

Archie hesitated, then nodded.

Naomi exhaled, then smiled. "I'm relieved," she said. "It's hard for me to accept that defending yourself is okay. Your grandpa might have been right about that Bible stuff."

Archie smiled back, his eyes shining. For the first time, Naomi saw not just her little boy but a young man learning to navigate the complexities of life. It was a milestone, a moment of unity wrapped in the wisdom of age and the innocence of youth.

As they drove back home, Naomi thought about the evolving dynamics of her family, a bittersweet mixture of stubbornness, love, and life lessons.

STRAWBERRIES

This is a tale about how we were and, perhaps, how we'd—secretly—like to be again. I hope it helps readers rediscover what was innocent in us all.

~ ~ ~

The sun shone through the kitchen window. The smell of coffee hung in the air. Isobel turned the page of the Sunday newspaper. It made a soft rustling sound. Her gaze traversed the articles, stopping at an advert about halfway down.

"Bora," she said, "there's a sale on manure at the garden shop."

Bora stopped scrolling through the travel destination photos and looked up from his mobile device. "Did you want me to get a bag when I drive past?"

She smiled. "It's at a good price."

He nodded. "Consider it done." He went back to scrolling.

Their son, Luka, who was sitting at the table eating a bowl of muesli, asked, "Why are we buying manure?"

Isobel turned the page. "To put on our strawberries."

Luka closed his mouth. A bit of milk dribbled from one side. His gaze darted between his parents. "Can't we just have cream and sugar on them?"

CHARCOAL GREY CLOUDS

Based on W. Somerset Maughan's quote about death in Samarra, this is my take on his message. We may all have something to do in "Worchester," but there's no hiding from fate. Destiny will find each of us.

~ ~ ~

C laudia offered her cheek to her husband while she dried her hands on a towel beside the sink. Claudia was in a mid-level management position at a Boston-based insurance company and had arrived home some time ago.

Karl brushed her brown hair to one side and kissed her.

"I was wondering where you were. I was about to message you."

Karl placed his car keys and briefcase on the smartly renovated kitchen counter. He moved to the center of the room so the kitchen table separated them. His tall, gangly appearance gave him the look of a dangling puppet. He bowed his head.

Claudia could see she wouldn't like what he had to say.

"I stopped to see Elżbieta on my way home."

Claudia leaned against the timber table; she had finished arranging a few pillowy cheese wedges on a cutting board. She picked up the serving knife like a street fighter and waved it toward the refrigerator. "I've got a bottle of Riesling chilling. Pour us a glass."

He did as he was told, trying to avoid her gaze as he shuffled towards the fridge.

She reached for her glass. "You've got some explaining to do."

He removed his sport coat, hung it over the back of a chair, and gently gripped her arm.

Claudia stopped. Her gaze fell to his shaky hand. She swallowed. "What did you do?"

He went to speak, but something prevented the words from coming out.

She ran her fingers around her glass's stem and breathed. "Not another argument with the departmental head? You can't afford to lose *this* job. We're just starting to get back on our feet."

He loosened his tie and sat in the chair. "No, nothing like that."

"You didn't bet on the horses again? Please, tell me you didn't."

Karl cleared his throat, swallowing a mouthful of wine. "I didn't."

Unable to hide her disgust, Claudia lent across the table and demanded, "Well, why did you see *that* astrologer?" The pain was on her face. "You promised it was over with her."

Karl's throat bobbed. "I wasn't successful with my bid for the advertising account. Long story, but I thought Elżbieta might be able to give me some insight into. . ."

Claudia's head was shaking as she massaged her temples. "She's a witch!"

"Claudia, stop."

"No. I mean it." She folded her arms. "She's trouble."

Karl winced. "She's not the trouble. I'm facing real trouble from—"

She squinted. "From what?"

Karl tossed back the remainder of his drink and poured another. "Listen, I need to go to Worcester. I'll stay the night with my sister."

Claudia pointed the knife at him. "What's going on? Talk. Now!"

He rubbed the back of his neck. "I have an appointment. I'll stay with Ruth."

Karl unbuttoned his top button, and with his eye on the door, he gulped the last of his wine. He stood, walked to the counter, and scooped up his keys. Then, like a marionette being jerked on its strings, Karl lurched towards the door, his arms flailing as he went.

Claudia placed her hand over her mouth, her gaze fixed as the door swung closed.

Through the window over the sink, Claudia watched the headlights of Karl's car fade as he reversed down the driveway. In the distance, charcoal-grey clouds formed.

* * *

The cutting board of cheese remained uneaten. The bottle of autumn harvest wine was empty; the last drops were sitting in Claudia's glass.

It worried her what Karl might say to Ruth. She didn't want her sister-in-law to think they'd argued. Ruth had taken Karl's side all his life, however senseless her younger brother was. She swirled the wine, watching the colors merge as she picked up the phone.

"Hi, Ruth. Thanks for accommodating Karl. He left in such a hurry he forgot his jacket and briefcase."

"What do you mean?"

"Isn't he there?"

"No, I haven't spoken to him since the weekend."

"Oh, he said he had an appointment and would stay with you rather than drive back. Perhaps he had a change of plans." Claudia tried to keep her voice from becoming shrill, "Sorry to bother you. I should have tried his number first. Thanks." She pressed the end-call button.

When she rang Karl, his cell phone rang out, and she grimaced, but her expression quickly turned to an unforgiving squint. She tapped Elżbieta's phone number into her device. There was a buzz, and she heard the astrologer's gravelly voice. Although they never met, Claudia imagined her to have raven black eyes.

"What did you tell Karl? He looked dreadful when he got home."

Elżbieta said in an Eastern European accent, "I tried to explain, but he became unsettled."

Claudia pressed her mouth to the phone. "Explain what?"

"He needs to stay home. All will be fine in the morning."

Claudia paced the kitchen floor. "Talk straight. I don't want to hear any 'eye-of-newt,' 'toe-of-frog' hoodoo. What did you say to him?"

There was a pause. "Death's looking for him."

Claudia's chest began to heave. "Death!"

"He doesn't understand. I tried to explain, but he rushed off."

"You are a sorceress stirring a boiling cauldron. First, you feed him nonsense about winning at the races; his gambling nearly bankrupted us. Now you're peddling unbridled fear. Shame!"

Elżbieta ignored her outburst. "I need to speak to Karl. Please put him on."

Claudia placed her hand on her hip. "You can't. He's not here."

"Huh? Not there? Where is he?"

Claudia felt as if a cold wind had blown in. She stood motionless. Her complexion became ghost-like. With tension in her voice, she said, "He went to Worcester to stay with his sister."

"Worcester"? Lowering her voice to a whisper, she said, "That's where his appointment is with Death."

RICHTER'S PROPOSITION

This story is based on "The Prisoner's Dilemma." It is a paradox that demonstrates how two people might not cooperate even though cooperation would be in their best interest.

~ ~ ~

The smell of incarceration was a dank odor of men who didn't shower. The rancid stench filled his nostrils as the shackles of the handcuffs tightened. The guard's heavy breath blew against the back of his neck as he leaned close to secure the cuffs. The sensation made Józef Jankovic's flesh crawl.

The guard was a middle-aged working-class man with a head like a bowling ball. He looked like he did body building in his off-hours. He whispered, "You're going down, and the guys next door are going to love your company." He paused. "And so will we."

It wasn't the words that seemed to have the impact—it was the way he said it. Bitterness? Hatred? Sadism? It was impossible for Jankovic to know. But for whatever reason, the guard decided to let Jankovic know   the

My version of this famous paradox was first published in 2014 by Lizard Skin Press (South Australia, pp. 43–57) in *Short Story Anthology 2* under my Oliver Yardley pseudonym. I also adapted as a stage play: Oliver Yardley, *Paradox of Trust: A One Act Play* (South Australia: Bibliologica Press, 2019).

sentenced prisoners in the next year expected him, Jankovic didn't reply.

He made it a habit not to say anything. And hadn't said anything during the investigation that landed him in custody. If he didn't talk, the burden of proof was with the state. There was no way he would help them send him to jail.

The guard pushed Jankovic forward toward the custody yard's barrier door. He stood there draped in a one-size-fits-all gray prison uniform. He shuffled forward under the force of the guard's shove, stood in front of the barrier as all felons do while they wait for the screw to open the door from the other side.

The custody yard was painted an insipid green. Perhaps it was the idea of some social worker who once read an article noting that green was a calming color. Who knew, but the appearance made the place look like some low-rent boarding house of years gone by.

The guard behind him walked around Jankovic's left side and stood in front, staring him down. The guard's bad teeth were smiling a false grin. His muscles pressed hard against the newly pressed shirt of his uniform, which seemed to be a size too small—perhaps to add *exaggeration* to his body mass.

With his knuckles, the guard reached behind and banged against the steel plate of the door. "The good doctor for a visit," he said as if he was talking to Jankovic, but he was speaking to the guard on the other side—his words were prison shorthand for, 'It's okay to open.'

Presently, there came the jingle of keys, then the clatter of a single key entering the lock. The thud of the bolt being withdrawn back into the lock could be heard, freeing the door. As the barrier swung open, Jankovic thought, *Free!* That's what he wanted to be…free.

The guard on the other side of the barrier stood with one hand on the key, the other on the top half of the door's frame. He had the toe of his leading foot pressed hard against it. His stance showed that he was prepared for any felon who might be so bold as to try and push the barrier open and rush past. And this guy wasn't going to let that happen. Whoever came through that barrier was under his control, and he established that as soon as he opened the door.

The barrier guard checked Jankovic over to ensure that he was cuffed and then nodded to the custody yard guard. Jankovic was shoved through, and as soon as he was out of the yard and in the walkway, the guard used his foot to force the door closed, making a solid thud as his wrist turned the key at the moment it closed. The combination of these things sent an echo through the adjoining cell block loud enough that other prisoners could hear. It was a clank that enforced the notion that when you were in there, you were there until *they* let you out. It was a fatalistic noise that took away choice. The choice to be free.

Józef Jankovic wasn't used to these sounds, or the smells, or the baggy clothes that dozens of previous prisoners wore before him. The thought of wearing another's shabby attire made him feel dirty. *Unsanitary.* He was more accustomed to choosing where he went, how he dressed, and how he got there. Like whether he was to go to Hong Kong for business, Abu Dhabi for shopping, London, or New York for pleasure.

As a person who worked in the comfortable world of international finance, a jail was not on that list of places to go or stay—ever! But Jankovic was on his way to make a choice. He had a visitor. His lawyer advised him that Detective Sergeant Cameron Richter wanted to discuss the charges on which he was held.

Jankovic was convinced that that meant the charges would be dropped. He couldn't believe that the judge had allowed the police to hold him without bail at the outset. Even his lawyer couldn't believe it. *Anyway, Richter coming into the jail meant they couldn't hold me any longer.*

Jankovic always stood straight—his lean physique and lightly tanned body a sign of a lifestyle that allowed for personal trainers and regular massages—but the craving of being able to beat the cops gave him cause to stand tall today. He could feel the gaze of some of the other prisoners narrowed on him from the barred cell windows above the walkway as he moved from the custody yard barrier across the long, narrow expanse to the adjacent building that housed the visitors' center. Those who watched from the surrounding cell blocks were the sentenced prisoners who had no choice now.

Smug conviction filled Jankovic. *I am about to be freed.* And to no one in particular, *...and you can have these rags called clothing back.*

He couldn't imagine what Richter would say to explain how little evidence they had and how hopeless the cops' case was against him. Would he apologize, saying, *Sorry buddy, it's all been a terrible mistake. You can go now.*

"I doubt it," Jankovic muttered under his breath as he was nudged along by the guard's sweaty hand.

Thinking to himself, he imagined it would be more like some long-winded legal rubbish about the provisions of section something-or-other of *The Act*, which might end with words like *you better behave 'cause we're onto you*, or some other face-saving bravado.

Face saving! That's what it'll be. It's some legal nonsense that lets Richter save face. Okay, I'll let 'em do that if it means I'm out of here. Once I'm out, I'll make my way to the airport; then they'll never see me again.

Jankovic continued across the walkway toward the visitors' center, the big barrier guard behind him at every step. With each stride, he gained comfort in the thought that by sunset, he'd be in the airline's business lounge enjoying a glass of Shiraz while he awaited his flight.

I'll pack straight away. I'll log onto my bank account and transfer the remainder of the cash from my offshore holding to the account in Belize. And I'll use the same alias to log onto the airline's website to book a flight in that name too—his thought was interrupted by the voice of his escorting guard when they reached the entrance barrier of the visitors' center.

"Over there, Doctor," he said with more than a hint of sarcasm, indicating that Jankovic stand in the alcove formed between the walkway barrier and the visitors' center meeting room. "You know the routine—get your gear off," he added, reflecting a total indifference to what was about to happen to Jankovic.

This meant that he needed to undergo a body search before he was able to enter the contact visit center.

A few minutes later, humiliated from having some alpha male run his rubber-gloved hands over his body— powerless to protest the intrusion—Jankovic consoled himself that he'd be out by sunset. *All I have to do is let them have an out to save face, and as long as I keep my mouth shut, I'm free.*

Richter was talking to his lawyer at a table at the edge of the room. The visitors' center was a large open room with white walls and bright fluorescent overhead lights reminiscent of a factory. It was a stark place designed for observation, not close, intimate conversations. The two men he was about to join looked like they were feeling relaxed, and their body language confirmed this. It looked like the two would have been at home in the pub's front bar, sharing a drink and a story about the night before.

But Jankovic approached them it was as if a siren went off, signaling that the two needed to turn their minds to business.

Simon Wellings, his lawyer, lifted his gaze and smiled at him as he advanced on the table. Wellings, dressed in a tailored black Italian suit, extended his hand and greeted Jankovic with a "How are ya, buddy?"

But his toffy private school accent wrapped in his designer menswear did not quite achieve the purpose of trying to sound like a regular guy. Nevertheless, he was attempting to establish that he was on his side. Jankovic appreciated the effort after what he experienced inside recently.

Then, turning slightly, Wellings motioned to Richter and said formally, "This is Sargent Richter," he paused, "from the fraud squad." But this time, he said it with all the weight his snobby accent could bear to underscore that he was there to represent *his* client.

How strange. One minute they are chatting as if they are friends, and the next, as if they were dueling with pistols drawn. Jankovic threw out his hand and forced a smile, but Richter, a large-framed, casually dressed man, simply held up his police ID, and with his other hand, indicated the chair, saying, "have a seat, this won't take long." There was no warmth in his voice—not even forced—and no emotion in his face.

Jankovic's reaction was, *what an arrogant prick.* His blood pressure rose as his anger peaked. He hated arrogance in what he saw as such an average man.

Jankovic had fixed Richter in a stare, and if his eyes were a laser, they would have burned a hole straight through him. But Richter didn't seem to care less.

He said matter-of-factly, "Listen up, Doctor, you have two choices: one, you give me a written statement admitting to the fraud, explaining the circumstances surrounding the embezzlement, or if you choose not to, you get ten years when the judge sentences you.

Jankovic was dumbstruck. He looked at his lawyer, who, too, appeared taken aback. Wellings turned to Richter and said with all the astonishment the two men were feeling, "What are you talking about? My client..."

Richter cut him short, holding his hand as if directing traffic. "It's your choice, but you'll do ten years if you don't provide me with your confession. It doesn't bother me either way. You're going to jail, but it's your call for how long." Richter leaned back in his chair, his trim, muscular physique and short cut hair reminiscent of a boxer throwing a challenge to an opponent.

Jankovic jumped to his feet, clenching his fists, beads of perspiration forming on his forehead. He wanted to punch Richter. He was staring down at Richter sitting at the table, Jankovic's heart bounding and face hot, when the visitors' center guard appeared, towering over him.

"Something the matter here?" His words were slow and deliberate. His presence was menacing along with the set of handcuffs he held at the ready.

Wellings said, "Nothing to worry about, officer. He was just looking for a pen to write me a note—I'm his legal counsel."

The guard took no notice of Wellings but kept his gaze on Jankovic while he relaxed his fists and sat.

Wellings cleared his throat to regain the group's attention, then turned to Richter. With an emphasis that projected a life of privilege, Wellings said, "You are distressing my client. What is it that you're doing?"

"I'm finalizing the case." The words came fast, hard, and cold.

"The case *is* finalized," Wellings stressed, "and we were expecting you to provide the details of the bail agreement so we can get my client out of this sewer and back into the community."

"Bail!" Richter said, half laughing and half shouting. It was loud enough to cause a few inquisitive heads in the visitors' center to turn.

"Yes, bail. So, what is this nonsense you are talking about? A confession!" Wellings' scorn for Richter's suggestion clearly showed in his tone.

Jankovic's contempt was boiling over, and he only wanted to smash Richter in the mouth. *Save face, he's off with the fairies.*

"It's all changed," Richter announced. He leaned forward toward the table as if he intended to punctuate his message. "You see, I found your companion."

He flashed a smile that would never have been strategic at a poker table. But it was obvious that he had no intention of masking his glee about the cards he held in his hand.

"What companion? Who?" replied Jankovic, vocalizing his disdain.

Wellings turned his head to address Jankovic. "It's best that I speak and see if I can understand what Detective Sargent Richter is on about." He faced Richter. "Detective, can you please explain."

"I found the other doc. Doctor Jeffery Davidson," he said flatly, the smile never leaving his face, his stare still fixed on Jankovic.

There was a stunned silence as they stared at each other. Richter's gaze turned to Wellings as if he wanted to see if the message sunk in, then twisted back to Jankovic. Richter's smile shifted to a demonic smirk as he crossed his arms over his chest and extended his legs. It was as if he had finished a large meal and was letting it settle.

Wellings liked to be in control—always. Jankovic had advised him that the co-accused—Davidson—was in a safe house in South Africa. His client told him that there was no way the cops would ever find him, let alone talk to him. *Richter had to be bluffing,* was Wellings' first thought, but he covered his emotional upset as best he could.

Nonetheless, Wellings, like Jankovic, also felt that his composure had faded and struggled to retain his temperament. He needed time to formulate a strategy, so he told Richter, "Why don't you tell us about Dr Davidson." His tone was measured, his eyes trying to show control, but he knew he was losing it—this had caught him by surprise.

But as soon as the words left Wellings' mouth, Richter fired back, "Immigration officials in Zanzibar caught him trying to get on a flight to Europe with a Zimbabwean passport." He paused and looked at Jankovic. "Not a smart move. It must have been a cheap forgery because they picked up on it straight away and held him for close to a month before he confessed to who he was. At that stage, he begged for consular assistance. You see, they 'persuaded' him to come clean, else they were going to deport him to Zimbabwe."

Richter stopped, looked at Wellings, and then continued, "That's only right, as that is what it said on his passport. But funny, he wasn't keen on that as an option. Didn't seem to want to go to his 'home country'." He paused again and, with a sneer, said, "I wonder why?"

It wasn't a real question—Richter knew the answer. Zimbabwe was in what seemed to be an endless cascade of civil and political violence. One could only imagine what would have happened to Davidson once he got off the plane at Harare airport and into the arms of the authorities there. The police were known to make arbitrary arrests and detain people to extract money. Davidson wouldn't have lasted a day, given his situation. And in prison with disease, rampant HIV/AIDS, no medical care, and lack of food and sanitation...

Richter let those thoughts sink in. Then he continued, "They called me, and I went over and talked to him. It was a long flight, and I had to make a few connections. But he's a nice guy. Beautiful country. I can see why tourism was such a big industry there. The beaches are white sand, and the water is a clear, deep blue. But too bad about the country's historical politics—ruined the tourism. Regardless, I can see why he went there to…hide."

After a brief pause, he went on, "I understand the two of you met at grad school—were enrolled in the degree of Doctor of Business Administration, he told me. Suppose that's DBA, huh?" He tilted his head. "Is that a real doctorate? I was once told that only PhDs were real doctors." His words trailed off as if he intended to belittle and provoke. Richter was on the attack again.

Jankovic looked up at the ceiling and then at Richter. *Yes, attack is the best defense.* He adopted Richter's strategy and, almost shouting, said, "bull shit"!

Without hesitation, Richter said, "Well, your legal counsel can verify that in the fullness of time, but right now, the issue is whether you are going to tell me everything or—"

Wellings interrupted with acid dripping from his voice, "Or else what—thumbscrews? Or some re-enactment of the Spanish Inquisition?"

"Or whether he's going to serve ten years in 'this sewer,' as you put it," said Richter.

Before Jankovic could respond, Wellings, in a superiorly polite voice, asked, "Detective, could you please tell us the basis for your assertion that my client will serve ten years? You have no evidence, and bail is imminent."

"Imminent!" Richter uncrossed his arms and leaned forward as if he were about to tell a joke at a picnic. "Perhaps, but not until ten-fifteen tomorrow morning at the bail hearing. Suppose I am unable to establish a prima facie case of embezzlement. In that case, you get one year at the minimum-security prison in the countryside for the lesser crime of larceny as an employee."

"Detective," said Wellings, "but we have gone through this already. You do not have more than circumstantial evidence, and as was borne out in the hearing earlier this week, a conviction for embezzlement is most unlikely, and we'll argue the larceny charge. What has changed?"

Richter sat upright in his chair and lifted a brow. "David-son." He emphasized each syllable as if the two other men were children being admonished.

"Pray tell? Inform us! How?" came Wellings' redress, his face turning serious as he waited for the next of Richter's salvos.

"I'll tell you what I told Davison the other day when I flew over to see him in jail," Richter said. "You have two choices. The first is to say nothing, like you have done all along. Your legal right." He glanced at Wellings and nodded in a mock acknowledgment of the Rule of Law. "But if you give me an honest admission about how you and Davidson pulled off the job, you'll be given immunity from prosecution as a witness for the State. Davidson, on the other hand, will get ten years in the 'big house'."

"And if my client maintains his innocence and continues to require the State to prove its case against him without providing you with your outrageous request to supply a statement of admission, then what—he does one year." Wellings pushed back into the chair's backrest in a display of counterfeit relaxation likely designed to unsettle Richter in his relentless attack.

"Not so," was Richter's retort. "If Davidson provides me with a statement instead, your client will be doing ten years, and Dr Davidson will go free."

Jankovic couldn't hold back any longer and blurted out, "But he won't!"

Wellings' hand shot out and grabbed Jankovic's forearm, squeezing it.

Richter was almost spitting out the words as he said, "Oh, you are the smart with numbers, Doc. Calculate this: the two of you are in the same situation. If the two of you remain silent, you both do a year for larceny as a servant. If one of you rats on the other, the one who confesses gets out of jail *free,* and the other does ten years in the big house up the road. If both of you confess, you both do five years.

"How confident are you that Davidson will remain silent so the two of you can do a year in jail and then walk? All he has to do is sing, and he goes free. Perhaps he'll go to Zimbabwe, or perhaps somewhere else a little more comfortable while you spent the next ten years in…this sewer, I recall it being described." He tilted his head at Wellings.

"Sure, but if my client provides information that might assist the prosecution and Dr Davidson does too, they both do five years," Wellings pointed out.

"Or your client doesn't, and he does ten years. Your decision."

"That is if Dr Davidson assists you…"

"Well, Mr Wellings, you and the accused have just one hour to decide. I either get a statement or we go to trial— that's what I'll instruct the prosecutor to tell the judge tomorrow. You take your chances on whether Davidson hasn't faxed me his statement in the meantime. If so, we'll advise the Zanzibar authorities to let him go free."

51

Richter eyed Jankovic. "What country are the funds in? Lichtenstein, Luxembourg, the Cayman Islands, Switzerland? I'm sure Davidson will wait for you so you can meet up there in…ten years and retrieve the money." And with that said, he let out a sarcastic chuckle.

Richter stood, shook Wellings's hand, and then said, "So, if I don't hear from you shortly, we'll see you at the trial opening next week. Your client will have the best seat in the house to view the proceedings." He then flicked his business card onto the table with the same arrogance he displayed when he flashed his ID.

Focusing on Jankovic still sitting at the table, he said, "Hey, the thought occurred to me—here we have a pair-of-docs in a paradox. Get it?" He snickered at his pitiful joke.

Without acknowledging Jankovic or Wellings, Richter spun abruptly and strode to the exit door.

Wellings watched as Richter's figure drifted across the room and vanished through the exit. He sat down and rubbed the back of his neck with a long, low sigh.

Jankovic was deep in thought but was presently interrupted by Wellings.

"Well, what do you want to do?"

Jankovic looked up and hesitated. In his various banking and investment deals, he had calculated probabilities before, but this was different. *How could a cop—a flatfoot beat plodder—have turned the odds against me?*

Panic was flowing over him, along with the smells of unwashed men, the sounds of slamming cell doors, and the sensation of handcuffs. *What the hell am I going to do?*

Those faces in the prison cell windows were vivid in his mind's eye now. The possibilities that ran through his thoughts were all dark. They were too terrible to contemplate.

Under the glare of the florescent lights, Wellings, with his manicured fingers, adjusted his silk tie and sat waiting for his instructions.

Jankovic's eyes were vacant, and as his posture sagged, he let out a whimper.

THERE'RE HUNDREDS OF THEM

People sit an exam and undergo a driving test when they first get their licenses. Then familiarity, complacency, and carelessness set in. As the years pass, some people can develop very bad driving habits. In this case, the driver is oblivious to his inattention.

~ ~ ~

The sunset bathed the freeway in an orange glow, its light reflecting off the vehicles speeding along the asphalt. The rhythmic hum of tires on the road and the gentle lull of the radio became a hypnotic background for Reginald's journey home.

"Hi darling, are you driving home?" His wife's voice, Edith, suddenly chimed in, crystal clear through the car's Bluetooth speaker."

Reginald smiled at her familiar tone, "Yes, darling."

"Where are you now?" Edith asked, concern evident in her voice.

"On the freeway near exit nine," Reginald answered casually.

Edith's tone suddenly changed, infused with worry. "Oh, dear! Please be careful. I just heard on the radio that some lunatic is on that stretch of the highway, and they are going in the wrong direction!"

"One lunatic—there are hundreds of them!" Reginald quipped.

SOMEONE I ONCE KNEW

In November 1983, the band Mondo Rock released Come Said the Boy. *It was a racy song about two young people exploring sex. For the teenage boy, it was his first time with a seventeen-year-old girl. Both were awkward with the situation. Despite these feelings, the lyrics tell how they tried to be sophisticated in each other's company.* Someone I Once Knew *is about a teenage boy who also tried to be urbane in the presence of a 17-year-old girl.*

~ ~ ~

I had the throttle open wide. If I twisted it any harder, the mechanism would've snapped. The only thing I could do to gain speed was to lean forward, flat across the handlebars. I had no idea about this racing stuff, but I'd seen competitors do it on television, and I was desperate— Walter was quickly pulling away from me.

But a minute later, I lost sight of him as he rounded a wide bend, so I let go of the accelerator and coasted back toward the speed limit. I was defeated but consoled my ego with the thought that *He was driving a Bonneville 650; I had a 350 Honda.*

I drifted into the turn, hoping to see Walter ahead of me, but no such luck. He must have hit one hundred. He was gone.

I returned to the upright position and slowed some more. I thought *He'll be at our usual meeting place and have to wait.*

It was a Saturday. Yesterday, high school finished for the summer. That meant all the seniors were celebrating. Those with one more year to go were restless, filling in the afternoon before we invited ourselves to *their* party. It was to be held in a vacant paddock tonight. Walter and I were all psyched up, spending the afternoon burning off energy and the rubber on our tires.

When I cleared the turn, a sedan passed in the opposite direction. It was a nondescript car, but what caught my eye was a girl looking out of the window, smiling, and waving a slow wave. Her facial expression gave me the impression that she had read my mind, saying, *Yeah, enjoy the party*.

It was spooky. I had to know more. My hand gripped the brake lever, and I did a bootlegger's turn. With all the 350 had, I throttled the bike through to fifth gear, pursuing the car around the sweeping bend and into the scrub outside of town.

When I had my front wheel a few feet from its rear bumper, I was relieved that my Honda could outperform an old family sedan. I flashed my light and sounded my horn. But the driver drove on.

Rather than risk head-on by pulling alongside it on the right, I rode up next to it on the left. It was a country road with no curb on the verge. When the driver saw me bouncing alongside her, she must have thought the chase was up because she signaled for me to get out of the way and brought the car to a stop. I cruised up close on the passenger's side, switched off my engine, and removed my helmet.

Five girls were inside—three in the back, two in the front. The front and rear windows were down, and in my mind's eye, I could only recall faces with beaming smiles. They said they had just graduated from the school in the neighboring district and were out having a good time.

Weren't we all!

Although I didn't say that I graduated—wow, these were *older women* to a seventeen-year-old—I think I just referred to the fact that I, too, had "finished." Hoping that I *finished* might lead them to believe I *graduated*...

Well, I must have been convincing because their questions flew at me as if it was speed dating (a phenomenon yet to be conceived, but for the record, I claim to have pioneered the concept at that encounter).

"What high school were you at?"

"What course did you study?"

"Do you know 'so-and-so'?"

"What kind of bike are you riding?"

It was like trying to drink from a fire hydrant. So many questions were coming at me that I was unable to respond.

That was until one of them said, "You've got green eyes."

With those words, the world ceased to be. Before, she was a face in a forest of faces. Now, she was the only thing I could see. I realized she I saw in the back seat their car passed.

My skin stretched as my face accommodated a grin, and I saw she was smiling, too. I leaned forward. "What color are yours?" I asked.

At that point, there was no sound. The questions had abruptly stopped. The other four looked on as if watching a movie at a drive-in.

Carol pushed toward me. I drew near to inspect her eyes. "They're green too," I said as if I had discovered some scientific unknown.

The warmth of her smile said *yes*.

I have no idea how it happened, but our faces drew nearer and nearer. We were free-falling into each other; nothing we could do could stop us.

I closed my eyes. Her lips touched mine. They were soft and gentle. I opened my eyes, and she brushed my lips again, her emerald eyes closing briefly to lock the moment away forever.

There was a chorus of gasps, and her friends fired questions at me again, but I had no idea what they were asking. Carol and I were in a tunnel, alone.

"What's your name?" I asked.

"Carol."

I told her mine and said, "There's a graduation party in that disused field next to the old grain silo tonight. Starts at seven. Will you come?"

I think she said she'd try, but her girlfriend, who was driving, had the only car. Her girlfriends wanted to go to the party of a "popular" guy at their school.

My shoulders drooped as I watched their car drive away. I can't recall the make or model, but I can still see it, vaguely, motoring on that two-lane road through the wooded area toward the town center.

That night, I waited at the edge of the field, my gaze darting from one carload of kids to another as they began arriving. I rubbed my hands and rotated the band of my watch. Then, like the appearance of fireflies on a summer's evening, I saw Carol walking toward me. We greeted. She said she couldn't stay; her girlfriends were waiting to go to Mr Popular's party. She left. Before she did, she gave me a bouncy grin and said, "Thanks."

I suspect the truth was that she had a boyfriend, but she didn't want to say. I might be wrong; I just got that impression. Yet, for some reason, she waved at me, kissed me, and convinced her friends to stop by the field to say goodbye.

I often asked myself why she was on that back road that day and why I turned to follow her. Well, I certainly couldn't follow Walter... Was it fate or a mystical attraction associated with the alignment of the moon and the stars?

In the following years, I asked anyone I met who attended her high school, but no one seemed to know Carol.

Still, I thought about our kiss and wondered whether our emerald eyes would ever meet again.

They never did.

DELIRIUM

At first glance, this is a humorous tale about an unlikely situation. Or is this what psychiatrists face with some referrals?

~ ~ ~

The psychiatrist's office was adorned with soothing artwork, casting a calm ambiance over the room. Dr Dorethy Reynolds, a a young woman with a kind smile, sat across from her patient, Mr Thompson.

Dr Reynolds glanced at the referral letter. "So, Mr Thompson, our doctor's referral letter says you have problems sleeping."

"Yes, that's right," Mr. Thompson confirmed, his voice laden with weariness.

Dr Reynolds leaned back in her chair, pondering for a moment. "I'm not sure why he asked me to see you— I'm a psychiatrist; I would have thought you should see an insomnia specialist."

Mr Thompson shrugged. "Oh?"

Dr Reynolds nodded. "Nevertheless, you're here. Tell me why you can't sleep."

A heavy sigh escaped Mr Thompson's lips. "It's my wife. She thinks she's a car."

Dr Reynolds raised an eyebrow, intrigued. "*She* thinks she's a car? What does that have to do with you not sleeping?"

"Because she sleeps with her mouth open," Mr Thompson explained, exasperation evident in his voice.

Dr Reynolds leaned forward; her curiosity piqued. "What does that mean, she snores?"

Mr Thompson shook his head. "No. It's the interior light. It keeps me awake."

NEWCOMB'S DAUGHTERS

This is a short story written with an epistolary element. The name of the story—Newcomb—refers to a thought experiment known as "Newcomb's Problem." It is a predicament involving two people with one who can foresee the future. The circulatory logic presents an unsolvable problem.

~ ~ ~

Helen footsteps on the small gray stones made a grinding sound as she stepped out of her car. Through the living room window, she could see her fraternal twin sisters, Sophie, and Ruby. She met their gaze as she approached the front door.

Tears welled in Sophie's eyes, then ran down her cheeks in a gentle parade of sadness.

Ruby pulled out a tissue from her jeans' pocket. "Hey girl, pull yourself together."

Sophie smiled but continued to dab her eyes as she made her way to the door. When it opened, she threw her arms around Helen, hugging her to the point where she couldn't move.

Ruby's greeting was more formal. After all, she knew Helen wasn't big on emotional displays. Sophie knew it too but wore her heart on her sleeve.

Taking off her black leather jacket, Helen said, "Where are you up to with packing the house?"

"Haven't got far," said Sophie. "It's more difficult than I thought." She exploded into sobs.

Helen gave her a harsh squint.

Ruby held Sophie's hand as she led her into the living room. The two collapsed into the soft pastel-colored cushions on the sofa. She offered Sophie another tissue.

After a few minutes Sophie regained some of her composure. Fighting back her sniffles she asked, "Was the flight, okay?"

As if she was reading a product label, Helen reported, "Yes, arrived on time, rented a car. Did it all online. All was ready for me at the airport."

"Was the road from the airport backed-up?" Ruby was instinctively trying to buy time for Sophie to compose herself.

Helen straightened her blouse. "No accidents, no construction. A quick drive."

"It was good of you to come back so soon after Dad's funeral," thanked Sophie. "I couldn't face it alone." She paused and corrected herself. "I mean Ruby's here—I'm not alone—I mean, I needed *you* too." Her eyes welled with tears.

Helen's eyes narrowed as she pursed her lips. Perhaps her lack of sympathy was because she could recall the practical jokes, pranks, and riddles their father played on his daughters over the years. All the time, he thought them funny. Helen thought otherwise. Nevertheless, her snub caused Sophie's shoulders to droop, her head to hang.

"What have you done so far?" Helen's question was dry, wanting to keep her sentimental sister focused on packing rather than their father's passing.

"Sophie's working on the kitchen; I'm doing the living areas. Perhaps you could do Dad's bedroom. There're some clothes Jack might like—the silk ties Mum bought Dad."

"Then we can all do the den. The size of his book collection will need all of us," said Sophie.

Helen rolled her eyes. "Who'd want a pile of old magic books, magazines on fortune telling and paranormal nonsense." She tossed her jacket over a chair and with dragging footsteps, she made her way to the rear of the house and the master bedroom. It was the room was where her father—Lance Newcomb—slept alone for years after their mother's passing.

Helen started with his chest of drawers. They were neat and tidy arrangement of sweaters and other garments— pressed shirts, Oxford button downs, turtlenecks—all in classic colors, patterns, and styles. These stirred no desire in her. She decided to give the contents to charity and abruptly closed the drawer.

Helen sat on the bed and looked around the room, her gaze searching for the next item in her triage. She realized Sophie wasn't capable of doing the packing herself, and Ruby would just pander to her sentimentality.

Helen reached across to the mahogany bedside table and opened the drawer. There was an odd assortment of writing pads, pencils, and a flashlight her father kept for emergencies. She made a mental note—these would go in the trash.

Her gaze settled on her father's wardrobe. She stood, moved to the door then opened it. On the back of the door hung the silk ties their mother bought Lance Newcomb— a stock market investor, entrepreneur, and self-made multi-millionaire. He enjoyed working out probabilities and people's intentions, so the stock market was the perfect forum to test his prophecies. He had once said he knew what people thought. And his bank balance suggested he was successful at doing it.

Shaking her head, Helen let one with an orange floral patterns run through her fingers and fall to the floor. These too would go to the charity thrift shop. She couldn't imagine her artist husband, Jack, wearing a tie.

Then she noticed her father's shoes. They were stacked neatly in boxes on the low shelf of the closet. Her father didn't have many—he was a frugal man even though he had enough money to own a shoe factory—but the few he had were stored in their original boxes. Lifting the lid to one confirmed they were polished before being put away.

She turned up her nose and pushed the box back in. Charity.

However, her attention was drawn to a gray steel box slightly larger than a shoe box that was positioned at the bottom of the wardrobe.

She looked at it closer. It was a safe. There was no handle or combination dial, just a slot for what looked like an old skeleton key.

For the first time since she arrived, she smiled. Hoping Ruby or Sophie were listening, she yelled, "Hey, I thought Dad's safe was in the study."

There was no answer, but she could hear her sisters walking down the hallway. The footsteps were purposeful, not the stampede-like roar the two made as kids when she chased them down the passageway pretending to be a ghost.

Ruby appeared at the bedroom door first. "What are you talking about? And what are you doing on the floor?

You haven't even started sorting things out."

Helen didn't answer, she simply pointed to the safe in the wardrobe. By this time Sophie was standing next to Ruby, "That's not a very big safe. What's in it?"

Resisting to state the obvious, Helen grimaced. "Needs a key. Where're Dad's keys?"

"I have them in my bag." Ruby hurried off to retrieve them.

When she returned, she had a large ring of keys.

Helen searched the ring, then held up a silver latchkey upright between her forefinger finger and thumb. "Here we go!"

As Helen inserted it into the lock, Ruby said, "I saw that key but thought it was some good luck charm Dad found in a second-hand shop. I thought those kinds of locks disappeared last century." She chuckled.

Helen admonished her, "Of course not."

The lock clicked. The device's bolt was released. Helen pulled, and the door swung open. The three stared into the safe.

She pointed with her index finger. "A book? Figures, he has books everywhere. Now we find a book in his safe." She rose, curling her lips.

Sophie grabbed the book. "What's this doing in there?" Her focus was on the binding. Rubbing her hand over the cover she said, "It's different."

It had creamy white pages and a tightly drawn, thin brown leather cover. It was an expensive looking book.

Helen seized the book from Sophie and thumbed through a dozen pages. "Their blank. Every page is blank." She pushed it into Ruby's hand.

Ruby flipped to the first page and there in their father's handwriting was a memo. She showed it to Sophie, who said, "This is a journal."

Helen snapped, "We'll never make any progress. Just put it in the den, and we'll deal with later."

Ruby extended her arm with the notebook held purposefully as if she were sharing her favorite childhood toy.

Helen glanced at the page, immediately noticing the writing was different from the writing pads beside his bed. She stared at it but wouldn't take it. But Ruby held it out. "Take it. Read it," demanded Ruby.

"No!" Sophie blurted out, trying unsuccessfully to snatch the book. "We aren't voyeurs!"

"Settle down," said Helen. "We need to. There may be information we should know."

Ruby clasped her hands to her chest. "Like confirmation that *I* was the favorite child."

Helen gave her an icy stare.

"You never forgave Mum and Dad for having a second child." Ruby's voice began to waver as she said, "Admit it, you wanted to be the only child."

As a child, Helen teased her sisters and never missed the opportunity to do so as an adult. She wagged her finger at Ruby and Sophie. "I didn't mind the family having one more, but then *you two* came along."

Ruby's eyes narrowed. "You know, when Mum said that she didn't have a favorite, it meant that she did, and that it wasn't *you*." She held up the book. "Anyway, we need to read this before we do any more."

Sophie fidgeted. "Are we allowed to read it? Looks like an instruction to someone. Isn't *that* personal?"

Helen moaned. "Of course, it's all right."

"Are you sure? What if he talks about things kids shouldn't know?" asked Sophie.

"You're an adult!"

"I know, but we're still his *kids*—do we need to know our father's thoughts"? Sophie said as she sat on the bed, sinking into the quilt.

Ruby propped herself up against the bed's headboard close to her sister.

Sophie patted Ruby. "This feels like when we were kids. Remember Dad reading us stories? We'd huddle under our blankets in bed."

Helen folded her arms across her chest and tapped her foot. What she was recalling was a different image—a picture of her father with a devilish grin, making up bedtime stories instead of reading the words. He'd created his own version of things based on the girls' likes or dislikes. It was part of his trickeries. Sophie loved it, but Helen never engaged. Ruby became bored with his antics and would fall asleep.

Ruby opened the cover to reveal the page with the neat handwriting. She looked at her sisters—Sophie face started to tic.

Helen still had her arms folded but was now frowning. "Go ahead. Read."

Ruby looked at the page, cleared her throat then began to read aloud.

At some stage soon, you will go to see my lawyer, Philip Allen, Esquire for a reading of my Will.

"See," scolded Helen, "I told you we needed to read this."

"Just be quiet and let me read."

His reading will inform you that in addition to my Will, there is a Codicil.

"Typical," interjected Helen. "There always had to be something else with him."

Ruby looked up. "Are you going to let me finish?"

Helen sighed. "Go ahead."

The three of you need to collectively, and unanimously, choose to have as your inheritance what the Will stipulates and *what is cited in the Codicil.* Or, *just what's in the Codicil.*

Helen made a hand gesture. "Well, there's not much to think about there. We take both."

"But," continued Ruby,

The Codicil could offer either a promise of $10,000,000, or nothing. I'm not telling what it holds, but I can say that my prediction will match your choice, and I'm never wrong.

Ruby looked at Sophie who swallowed and bit her lip.

Helen scowled. "What's he playing at now?"

"It's Dad. He was always like that," said Sophie.

"He's dead, and he's still playing as if we're interested in his fortune cookie magic," huffed Helen.

Correcting her, Sophie pointed out he was interested in

statistics, Sudoku, and cryptic crosswords.

"More like astrology, horoscopes, and mystic hocus-pocus."

Sophie pursed her lips before saying, "They were brain teasers."

"Oh, yes, you were his favorite. You and he would work them all out."

Ruby held up her hand. "Stop you two! I never gave his sorcerous monologues much credence, but these next lines might be an omen. Listen."

With an almost unnatural stillness, she finished,

If I predict that you will take both options—the Will and the Codicil—then all you get is what's in the Will; the Codicil will contain nothing.

If I predict that you will choose only the Codicil, then $10,000,000 will be added to your inheritance.

But here's the challenge—if I predict that you'll choose the Codicil only, but you select both, you'll receive $10,000,000 plus what's in the Will.

Finally, if I predict the Codicil only and you select this option, you get just the $10,000,000, not what's in the Will.

Unable to remain silent, Helen blurted out, "Oh spare me. He must think we really believe his tea leaf readings."

Sophie held her head high and in a slow voice said, "He read coffee grounds, not tea leaves. Gypsies read tea leaves; the Turks and Greeks read coffee grounds."

Clutching Sophie's arm, Ruby said, "Well, whatever he was reading he concludes with this."

If you select at random—toss a coin—then be warned,

I'll have predicted that you will have done that, and the Codicil will contain nothing.

Helen waved her hands in a circle above her head. "Isn't he missing the part where he says 'Abracadabra'."

Rigid, Ruby cocked her head. "Did I just read *that*?"

"Yes, you did. And the two of you should have taken what Dad said about tasseography more seriously," said Sophie.

For a few minutes, Helen and her sisters argued about what the note meant and whether it was genuine.

When they agreed it was what it purported, Helen winced. "The way I see it is we have two logical approaches to this: regardless of what Father predicted, opting for both—the Will and the Codicil—will give us the most benefit."

Ruby gasped. "What? I don't understand how you came to that conclusion."

Helen slowly paced. "Listen, if he predicted we selected both, it's a case of choosing between what's in the Will—by taking the Will and the Codicil—and nothing—by just taking the Codicil. Don't you see? By taking both, it's far better."

Ruby said, "I'm not sure. Aren't we doing what Dad says he predicted we'd do?"

With tension rising in her voice, Helen snarled, "Do I need to get out my old Crayons and draw you a picture? Think about it; even if he predicted we'd only take the Codicil, then opting for both could give us the $10,000,000, plus what's in the Will, whereas taking only the Codicil would just give us the $10,000,000. Don't you understand? Taking both is better—it doesn't matter what he predicted."

Ruby sighed. "You make sense, but there's another possibility. By opting for the Codicil only, we might be better off."

"No way," said Helen.

"Hear me out," said Ruby. "We'd be silly to discount the possibility we could either get *nothing* or what's in the Will, plus the $10,000,000. That's because both these possibilities require Dad to have predicted incorrectly. But he says that he won't be wrong in his prediction, so we'd be better off choosing between what's in the Will—select both—or the $10,000,000 by selecting the Codicil. So, you see, taking the Codicil only is better."

Sophie was sitting quietly against the pillows, slowly rubbing her hands.

Helen and Ruby turned to her.

With a huff, Helen said, "You're the only one to have worked out most of Dad's—" She smiled a gentle smile, and in a soft, placating voice said, "—brain teasers. What do you think?"

"I thought you said his hobby was just hocus-pocus. That tasseology was mystical. Now you want my opinion?" With her hands folded across her chest, she said, "Does that mean you think I'm a fortunate teller?"

Helen's face turned red. The veins in her neck protruded. She went to open her mouth, but Ruby swung her leg off the bed and stomped on her toes.

Sophie raised her chin in defiance. "I'm happy with what's in the Will. Or nothing. We can follow your reasoning or Ruby's. Doesn't matter to me."

Ruby had enough. She stood, then faced Helen with her nose almost touching her sister's. In a deep voice, carefully pronouncing each word, she whispered, "Be nice to her, or I'll pull your carrot-colored hair out."

Helen stepped back and forced a smile. "Sophie, darling. I've been so saddened by Father's passing I've been insensitive to you. I don't know what has gotten into me. Won't you give it some thought as to how we solve this conundrum? What would Dad have predicted? Please? Clearly, Ruby and my solutions have flaws. We need *you* to solve this circular logic of his last puzzle."

Sophie turned toward the window. Stared into the distance. Her right cheek started to twitch.

Ruby looked at Helen and shrugged. They waited in silence.

When Sophie tuned back, her gaze was alert. Her fists were clenched. "Make me a ground coffee…"

THE DICK

There are good, bad, and people who behave ugly in this world. If we haven't been in the situation of this story's protagonist, one day, we might. Faced with his dilemma, what would you do? I know what Detective Sergeant Harper did...

~ ~ ~

There's a host of sayings that warn against acting badly to others: "What goes around, comes around"; "You reap what you sow"; and "Every dog has its day." They're all forms of wishful thinking—hope. Hope that the forces of the universe—karma—will come to bear on those who haven't played fair.

I never gave these home-spun philosophies much credence. But when my phone rang that morning, I had a flash that his fate was about to be delivered to me.

As a cop, I'm not one to be startled, but my breath caught when I heard his voice. He announced his name as if I wouldn't remember him. It's odd how you can recall a person's voice after years. Like listening to Billy Holiday—it's never forgotten. *I* knew who he was. And I remembered what *he* did to scuttle my promotion.

He said, " Collin Lynch, good to talk to you after all this time."

If insincerity was a liquid, it would have run out of my smartphone and short-circuited the device.

He cleared his throat, "I'm investigating an event about nine months ago when you were on the shift in the holding cells. Involves a prisoner claiming we stole his pool cue while locked up."

"Gee, you get all the good jobs."

He ignored my veiled sarcasm and went on. "This prisoner was only in for a few hours awaiting arraignment. So, according to standard operating procedure, his cue would've been put into the storeroom."

"And?"

There was a silence at the other end. He was a lieutenant, and I was a sergeant. Although we both had our detective ratings, he was technically my superior. I knew I was swimming in deep water by being flippant. He could've taken me to task, but I sensed he wanted something. His pause told me so. I guessed he was restraining himself because his reputation wasn't for being mild-mannered.

He gave a light cough. "Harper, I've got a problem, and I need your help to fix it."

Those words sounded the proverbial alarm bell. Word around the department was that he was bent. Two detectives in his former squad were fired for misconduct, but no hard evidence ever surfaced to cause Lynch grief. Rumor was he was in the "penalty box" doing "special investigations" after his unit was disbanded. I guessed he'd be there until management could get enough on him to force him out of the job.

"Me?" I went mute without adding the "...help *you*?" part of the sentence.

At his end of the phone, there was the sound of him shifting in his chair. He was a big man. I recalled him looking like he spent more time in a bar than where he should have been—on the street.

"Sure. Everyone helps everyone. Isn't that our ethos? The spirit of fellowship."

"Sounds like you are trying to convince yourself of that."

There was silence again.

I may have swum into the deep water with that remark, but I held steady. I didn't utter a word. I waited. All I could hear was his wheezing breath.

I could have kept up the game, but I had work to do. "Well, Lieutenant Lynch, I won't keep you from finding that cue stick. Really envious you get these 'special investigations'."

He exploded, "Listen, Harper, I'm not fooling around. They're trying to screw me. If I don't clear this backlog of paltry cases, they'll throw that frigging performance indicator crap at me."

I knew how to give the silent treatment too. So, when I thought just the right amount of time had passed, I said, "Why should that concern me?"

I heard a crash. His fist pounding on his desk? Whatever it was, I got the impression my answer wasn't to his pleasure.

"Think about this, Sergeant Harper." If his words were bullets, they would have been armor-piercing. "There's a reason you never got that job you applied for in *my* squad."

"Lieutenant, *you* don't have a squad anymore. Remember? You're doing 'special investigations' now."

"Your problem, Harper, is you're a frigging boy scout.

You know damn well what I'm asking."

I pressed my smartphone's voice recorder app, hoping what he was about to say would be fate's calling card. "No, Lieutenant Lynch, I don't understand what you're asking me."

"You were in the cells the night when that prick got arrested. I need a statement from you explaining what happened to his frigging pool cue. If I don't get that statement, I'll have to find his God-damn stick. And if you make me find it, I might shove it up your ass before I hand it back to him."

"So, you're asking me if I recall the events of that night, and if I do, you're asking me if I have firsthand knowledge of the missing article's whereabouts?"

"You're a prick. You going to do it or not?"

"First of all, Lieutenant, I'm not a prick. I'm a dick, and you know what? So are you. And being a detective, my training is to refer to my notes when I'm unsure about a specific event or conversation before making a statement. You know what else? I'm going to have to get back to you after I do."

I didn't need to terminate the conversation because I could almost feel the concussion of him slamming the handset of his desk phone.

I could see why he was in the penalty box. Even though I had his voice on an audio file, when I listened to it, there was nothing to suggest that the Internal Integrity investigators would be interested in it.

Reaching into my bottom drawer, I retrieved a handful of old notebooks, palm-sized pads bound in various colors, and each dated by month. I shuffled through a few, and then a few more until I found the one with the details of the prisoner's detention. I thumbed through the pages until I came across the entry for that night.

As I anticipated, I had noted that I relieved the two arresting officers of the pool cue, which was in the prisoner's possession when they arrested him. Following the department's SOP, I handed it over to the storeman, and we both logged it into the property store.

Then it came to me. The storeman put it in a locker. But the locker wasn't one of the department's—it was a locker being held in relation to another matter. I suspected that when that locker was handed back to the accused, the pool stick went with it.

I could have picked up the phone and given the lieutenant that lead, or I could have just read him want I recorded in my notebook.

If I gave him the lead, he could solve the mystery. But if I read him what I had written, he would likely be offered early retirement for failing to meet his performance indicators.

I wasn't a big fan when the department brought in these performance metrics. Now, they looked like a pretty good idea. I asked myself whether I should play fair with him or even the score.

It was a choice. A choice between doing what was legally required—check my notes and report what was fact or do the right thing—offer Lieutenant Lynch a lead to what likely happened.

The pool stick wasn't the problem; the accused would get it back, or the department would compensate him. The real issue was—did I spare the lieutenant by throwing him a lifeline?

Or, did I save my fellow officers, the department, the city that employed this dubious character, as well as the public, by letting him drift off into his own deep water on a raft named 'a poor performance review'?

I set my jaw and nodded. I picked up the phone, dialed, then hummed a tune while I waited for him to answer.

THE EXPANDING UNIVERSE

This story is based, somewhat in fact. Indeed, the fictional Mr Thomas is a construction of a natural person I once knew. He is a person who should remain in his prison hospital under the care of "Dr Neumann" or whoever is treating him forever for the good of society.

~ ~ ~

"Please take a seat, Mr Thomas."

"Thank you."

"Could you begin by telling the review panel about your progress?"

"Progress?"

"Yes, your progress. The panel is charged with reviewing your treatment program. The Parole Board wants reassurance that you're better before it releases you back into the community."

"Oh, I'm feeling fine. I take my new medication and follow my psychiatrist's instructions."

"Dr Neumann's case notes say that you're no longer experiencing the episodes you had a while back."

"I'm good now. The meds helped."

"Please tell the panel about Dr Neumann's cognitive

This tale was initially published by Celapene Press (Melbourne, Australia: pp. 73–74) in Katheryn Duncan, editor, *Short and Twisted, 2016*, under the nom de plume of Oliver Yardley.

therapy. Did the treatment assist you?"

"Sure. I thought the universe was doubling every few minutes. Caused me a lot of anxiety. Severe panic attacks. That's what made me do what I did. But now I realize it was all in my head."

"Please go on."

"As you know, I thought everything in the universe doubled, including the universe itself. I believed that you, me, and everyone in the world were doubling in size. So was everything in their lives—it was all doubling. The earth beneath our feet was doubling, the seas were doubling, and so was the sky. I thought that the moon was doubling, and the stars and the sun, and—"

"Yes, yes, we understand. It's described in Dr Neumann's notes."

"Could I have a glass of water, please? The meds make my mouth dry."

"Certainly."

"Well, Dr Neumann helped me work through the problem. Now, I understand how silly the idea was."

"That's good to hear. What are your thoughts about the universe now?"

"Oh, it isn't expanding. No. Not at all. We are the same size. Now I know that matter can't expand—double, triple, or even shrink. It's not physically possible."

"Dr Neumann helped you understand this?"

"Oh yes. I enjoyed my sessions with him."

"Well then, that about concludes our review. But before we adjourn to consider our recommendation, I have one last question. I've noticed that you've been snapping your fingers since you arrived. Do we make you nervous?"

"No, I'm fine. Your prison hospital doctors are nice."

"I'm pleased to hear that. But why are you snapping your fingers?"

"It's the only thing I found that works. And I have tried many things. But rest assured, this works."

"In what way?"

"It stops everything from shifting three feet to the right every few minutes."

"But, Mr Thomas, I thought—"

"No, no, no! This is different. Physics doesn't prevent objects from moving. There're physical laws that explain how objects move."

"I haven't noticed anything in this room shift. Everything is still where it was minutes ago."

"See, Doc, it works!"

ABILENE'S FOG

This story is about the morality of going along with the crowd: it highlights how being meek or submissive can have consequences. The paradox from which the story springs is an adaptation of the "Abilene Paradox." It is a story about a group that comes to a decision that is not in anyone's interest. Each person assumes their view contradicts the group's, so they don't want to be the odd person out by objecting. The basis of the paradox is that people want to fit in—submit to the will of the collective. Inspired by the 1972 Watergate Affair, my version of this story can be translated to other societal issues.

~ ~ ~

I fixed my stare on Bob Abilene. He was sweating; beads appeared on his forehead, causing the ends of his hair to twist into damp curls. He swayed in the police van as it negotiated turns and the traffic—so didn't the rest of us. But Abilene seemed to be in another world. His dark eyes were vacant.

The four of us must have looked out of place in our business suits with our hands cuffed in front of us on the benches that faced each other. Trying to maintain balance on the white plastic seats was difficult. The smell of body odor made me wonder what sorts of people occupied them before us.

The only light came from a small window at the top of the door at the rear that revealed the glow of the streetlights, and the neon shop signs we passed.

My eyes burned, and my head ached. I knew we hadn't

made any plans to get bail. We were supposed to have installed the listening devices and been out of the building in twenty minutes. It didn't turn out that way. A piece of tape on the door holding the lock mechanism gave us away.

My training in black ops taught me enough to know that any words I spoke while in custody could be overheard—and used against me. So, I scanned the inside of the van. I couldn't see anything suggesting a mic or a camera. Anyway, I wasn't likely to find one; after all, we weren't in Central America…

I leaned forward, "Will the Firm have a lawyer at the arraignment?"

Abilene rocked gently with that dazed look.

"Bob! The lawyer? Will the Firm have one at the hearing with the judge?"

He turned his head. Barely audible, he said, "The op was extra-legal."

"Extra-legal?"

He nodded and bowed his head.

I glanced at José Lorenzo, who was sitting next to him. Lorenzo's lips parted, but no words came out.

In her red, tailored jacket and heels, Ana Renaldo said what Lorenzo was likely thinking, "You mean the op wasn't sanctioned by the 'Top Floor'?" She threw a glance at Lorenzo.

He had that expression you give a friend when you want to leave a party early, except no one was leaving this get-together.

I pushed forward on the seat, my knees touching

Abilene's. "What the hell are you talking about?"

His' face looked like it was made of wax. "When I suggested the op, I didn't think any of you would follow through. I made the task exceedingly belligerent because I wanted *you* to dismiss the idea. Wanted *you* to be the weak ones for once."

I folded my arms. "So, when I said I'd go along, your bluff fell apart."

"No. At that point, I was counting on José or Ana to voice up."

Renaldo pushed me aside and then grabbed Abilene by the knot of his tie before he dragged him close. "You worthless turd! Do you know how hard it is for a woman in this game? I wasn't about being the one to talk down an op."

She gave his tie a quick yank, and like a flash of jagged light, slammed his nose into her forehead. As she did, the crack of cartilage being crushed shattered the interior. The impact opened a faucet of blood.

I thrust my cuffed-arms between them, forcing her back onto the molded seat. We passed a streetlight, and I caught a glimpse of crimson covering his business shirt.

Abilene cupped his hands around his nose. "You're the dipstick, Ana. If you had guts, you'd have said 'no' and be able to live with the decision."

Closing his eyes, Lorenzo laid his head on the backrest. He swayed sideways as the van turned a corner. "Rash, stupid, ill-thought-out. It was one of the dumbest plans I've ever heard." His gaze narrowed on Abilene. "I didn't want to dissent. Didn't want to show a lack of commitment. *I* should have been the one to say 'no-way'."

Abilene pinched the bridge of his nose. "I never counted on you 'musketeers' going ahead with it." He shook his head. "I should've known black operatives never do anything by half."

Abilene's face was caked with drying blood. "So," I said, "you suggested an op that couldn't succeed. It caused a fog, and, in that mist, we agreed, didn't want to let each other down even though we thought otherwise. And because no one—including you, Bob—had the courage to speak against our misguided view, we're now on our own. Disavowed."

The police van started to slow.

I bared my teeth. "What's worse, Bob? Talking about integrity, or living with the fallout because you didn't?"

The van stopped, and the door swung open. A detective sergeant in a pressed black suit and polished shoes looked in. He winced. "What the hell happened to him?"

BEYOND WHAT WE CAN SEE

Comparable to the biblical parables that stimulate deep reflection, this modern-day tale juxtaposes the quest for understanding the universe with a desire to comprehend the mysteries of faith. The story delves into the enigmatic nature of space and the intrinsic human drive to seek answers beyond what is readily observable.

~ ~ ~

With the sun casting warm rays through the taxi window, the courteous driver addressed the passenger in a respectful tone, "Good afternoon, ma'am. Where to?"

The passenger, feeling a mix of exhaustion and anticipation, responded, "Logan Airport, please."

The driver looked in his rear-view mirror and asked, "Busy day?"

The passenger sighed softly, "Yes, just finished presenting a paper at the cosmology conference. Heading home now."

Showing a genuine interest, the driver responded, "Cosmology, ah? My daughter is studying that. She wants to be a beautician. She dreams of having her own salon."

The passenger kindly replied, "That's nice. I wish her all the best. But I'm a cosmologist, not a cosmetologist. I study the universe, not beauty treatments."

Apologizing for the misunderstanding, the driver explains, "My apologies; I'm a bit hard of hearing. Traffic noises, you know." He paused, then continued, "The universe, you say. Is it true that a Black Hole will swallow the Earth?"

The passenger smiled, offering reassurance; her voice conveyed certainty, "Unlikely, and positively not within our lifetimes. Rest assured, we have more to explore."

Curiosity lingered as the driver inquired, "So, what do you study?"

The passenger responded with a sense of purpose, "I'm looking at whether space is infinite."

Eager to understand, the driver asked, "Well, is it? Is it endless?"

The passenger hesitated, her voice full of fascination and determination, "We can't be one-hundred percent certain. That's why I'm studying it."

Seeking further clarification, the driver wondered, "Can't you see the end of the universe with one of those telescopes?"

Regret seeped into the passenger's voice as she explained, "We can only see forty-six light-years away. At that point, we resort to *a priori* logic."

Intrigued, the driver inquired, "What's that?"

The passenger patiently elaborated, "It is a way of thinking that, although based on what we can observe, allows us to contemplate what is theoretical. Like whether space extends beyond forty-six light-years, and if so, how far."

Still seeking answers, the driver questioned, "If you're using that '*a priori*' thinking, why haven't you got the answer?"

A moment of contemplation follows before the passenger responds, "Here's the dilemma—suppose you could travel to the edge of space, that forty-six light-year boundary. While you're floating in space, you throw a baseball. What would happen to the ball?"

The driver pondered the scenario, uncertain, "Well, I can't say because I don't know if that's the end of space."

Affirming the driver's uncertainty, the passenger continued, her voice animated with excitement, "Exactly! Either the ball would be stopped by whatever makes up the boundary of space, which means there is something on the other side and space keeps going, or it will continue its flight."

Realization dawns on the driver, who muses, "In either case, wouldn't that mean that space is endless?"

A confident smile graced the passenger's face as she proclaimed, "That's what I asserted in my paper at the conference."

ABOUT THE AUTHOR

Dr Henry (Hank) W. Prunckun, BSc, MSoSc, MPhil, PhD, is a former government intelligence officer who spent twenty-eight years in various operational fields, including security, investigation, and counterterrorism. He is now an Adjunct Associate Research Professor with Charles Sturt University, Sydney, researching transnational crime, and the author of two dozen factual books on secret intelligence.